Options

Lucy Gladstone struck out again at the dating game. She was a virgin and, according to her mother, would destroy her chances of a good life that ended with going to heaven if she gave in to her natural desires.

Tom Whitecloud was living a few doors down a floor below. He was, unlike so many, beautiful!

Several girlfriends at work warned her that making an Indian her first would ruin her for other men. They would all seem so dull and inept.

She had several options. Follow her mother's advice, and probably die a spinster? Find a man to make a woman out of her? Take the extra chance that the one she wanted, Tom Whitecloud, would leave her wanting more than any man other than an Indian could deliver?

She couldn't hold out much longer. Which option would be best for her?

Mom's way was as much as out. Then Tom stopped her on the stairs as she was coming home from being dumped – again. It seemed, at times like these, that no man was interested in a second date with a girl who wouldn't put out.

About the author

CD Moulton has traveled extensively over much of the world both in the music business, where he was a rock guitarist, songwriter and arranger and in an import/export business. He has been everything from a bar owner to auto salvage (junkyard) manager, longshoreman to high steel worker, orchid grower to landscaper, tropical fish farmer to commercial fisherman. He started writing books in 1983 and has published more than 350 books as of January 1, 2023. His most popular books to date are about research with orchids, though much of his science fiction and fantasy work has proven popular. He wrote the CD Grimes, PI series, and the Det. Nick Storie series, Clint Faraday series, and many other works.

He now resides in Gualaca, Chiriqui, Panamá, where he writes books, plays music with friends, does research with orchids and medicinal plants. He has lately become involved in fighting for the rights of the indigenous people, who are among his closest friends, and in fighting the extreme corruption in the courts and police in Panamá.

He offers the free e-book, *Fading Paradise*, that explains what he has been through because of the corruption.

CD is the discoverer of the Chadam Protocol for curing cancer.

Facebook page Ambrosia peruviana for cancer.

Options

<u>*Options*</u>

Lucy Gladstone sighed heavily as she climbed the four flights of steep stairs to her dreary room.

Another night, another bust.

What the hell was wrong with her? Everyone said she was attractive and intelligent, but she had yet to have a second date with a guy. She could get the first date in two minutes, flat. It seemed guys wanted to date her, but that she did something that made them stay away. They all said they had a good time, and would call – then never did.

Maybe it was true, what Arlene said. Put out, or get used to it.

Weren't there any decent guys anymore? She was raised in a religious family, and was taught from infancy that good girls didn't even kiss a guy on the first date.

She had normal feelings. She had wanted to do a lot more than kiss a couple of them, but "knew" it would lead to something more, and a girl *must* be a virgin when she married, or she was common trash, and always would be. You can't unring a bell, and you can't unruin a woman.

It wasn't worth it! She was 19 years old, and had never been passionately kissed, even.

Was it true a man knew the first thing if a girl was a virgin?

Men were lucky. There was no way to tell if they were, and they were expected to use loose women. Even after they were married, they could get away with running around, most of the time, while a woman was a cheap whore if she even so much as flirted with another man after they were married. Her mother had repeatedly warned her about that. She had impressed upon her that sex was always a very special thing to a woman, but a man was different. It was only special with a woman he really loved. Other than that, it didn't mean anything but a good time to a man. That was a burden all women of all times must bear. A man who was hot would say anything, even tell a woman he loved her, but men were much closer to animals than were women, and had no control over such things. Once they started, they couldn't stop. That was true only with a small number of women.

Nymphomania.

She sighed tiredly again. Maybe, deep down, she wished she were a nymphomaniac. She fantasized about having sex with two or three men, sometimes.

How damned stupid! Maybe she would be like her mother, and not even like sex. Maybe it would be nothing more than a wifely duty, and she would end up wishing her husband – assuming she ever had a husband – would get a mistress so he would leave her alone.

Her father had a string of mistresses, and everyone in town knew it, except her mother. A lot of people made jokes about her father and women.

Maybe she knew it, and was glad of it. She as much as bragged about being frigid, like it was some kind of virtue.

She was spending far too much time thinking about sex. Now she would feel guilty about it. She was raised to feel guilty if she ever thought about it, but had rejected the whole religious bit.

Well, consciously, she had. It was still there, or she wouldn't be feeling guilty, right now.

Tom Whitecloud was just coming out of his apartment, and smiled at her. He'd made it plain that he would like to spend a little time with her, but she was almost terrified of him, because Arlene said that, once she was laid by an Indian, other men would seem dull and inept.

God! He was attractive! Those dark eyes bored

right through to her soul! He was so nicely built, too. "Built for sex," as Arlene said. She had spent a couple of nights with him, and said he was the best she ever had.

"Turning in early?" he asked.

"Yes, I have to work tomorrow, so ... to be honest, I just got dumped," she replied.

"Ah! Any man would be a total fool to dump such a beautiful, chaste, and warm woman!" Tom said, smiling.

"I'm used to it," she answered. "I think it's the 'chaste' part that runs men away."

"Ah! So the man is so stupid he doesn't know a sprinter loses the long race!" he said, chuckling low in his throat, and giving her a very obvious look. "Perhaps you should date a man who would rise to the challenge!

"It's early. I'm merely going down to the café for one beer. Perhaps you will do me the honor of joining me? I will ply you with alcohol, then seduce you, and you won't be chaste anymore. Your dates will then be competing with each other for your attention!

"Seriously, we can sit and talk. No more, but I will say before that I find you a fascinating woman, and I will probably try."

"That is refreshing! A man who doesn't say a lot of things to make a woman think he's ... I would very much like to have a beer, I think. I never have, you know.”

He smiled, and she felt a heat more intense than she’d ever felt before. “Then you will have a weak cocktail, not a beer,” he decided. “I will try to seduce you. Have no question about that!”

She couldn’t understand what she was feeling. She wanted to undress him, right there on the stairs. She wanted to *know,* and she wanted *him* to teach her.

She was also very afraid, as she said, “Perhaps you already have.”

He laughed low in his throat again, and she felt a warm tingling all over her body.

This was it! This was the night! She was going to be a woman, not a girl, in the morning. She wanted to tell him to forget the alcohol and seduction, she wanted to go back into his apartment, right now!

He knew. She saw it in his eyes. He smiled with those perfect beautiful teeth, and raised an eyebrow at her, and she almost fainted. She had never felt like this before, scared and excited and ... something else. Something new.

He waved his hand at the stairs, then at his apartment door, and raised the eyebrow again. She turned toward his door.

He opened the door, and waved her in. She

noticed her heightened sense of smell, and that the room smelled so different than her place. No perfumes or special scents. It was a very inviting place, and very masculine. She hadn't been inside, having only seen in a few times as she was passing. There was a leather sofa, with two unmatched leather chairs, and a long low coffee table with a TV/DVD on a smaller table, across the room. There was an old vinyl record player, and about a dozen records on a shelf below it on a bookcase/shelf to one side. She took that all in in a glance, and turned to smile up at him as he slid one hand around her waist and drew her to him to give her her first really passionate kiss.

It wasn't like on TV. They didn't claw at each other and breathe in gasps, or whatever, and they didn't start tearing each other's clothes off. It was soft and insistent, and she did cling to him.

What a silly thing to think of! She pictured herself unbuttoning his shirt – but it was just a tee shirt. A tight white tee shirt that showed off his beautiful, slender, muscular body so well.

He slid his other hand around her waist, and pulled her even closer. The kiss lingered, and she was actually beginning to breathe ... different. Heavier, and she was actually dizzy. She had her arms around his neck, then moved to place one hand on his waist. He kissed her again, lightly, and she ran the hand up under the tee shirt to his powerful chest.

His skin felt so warm and so good!

He led her to the couch, and laid back. She laid on top of him, and started to explore him. He smiled, and did a bit of exploring, himself. He slipped off the tee shirt, and she couldn't breathe! She couldn't believe how sexy his body was! She had seen him without the shirt, from a distance, and had noticed how nicely-formed he was, but this close, touching, was totally different.

He was unbuttoning her blouse, then pulled her closer and kissed the base of her throat as he slid one hand softly downward as he used the other to remove her bra. He smiled, and kissed her again, a longer, more intense kiss, but not the passionate panting type. She found she liked it this way. Very much.

She had opened his belt, and was unzipping his pants before she realized she was doing so. He unsnapped her skirt, and she slipped out of it as he removed his pants.

God! He was beautiful! She had never before been with a nude man, having only seen pictures, but he was gorgeous, and he was certainly ready.

He picked her up and took her to the bedroom. She laughed as he placed her on the bed, then climbed in, himself. She kissed him, then found herself nibbling at his chest. She had never known anything like this. She hadn't known it was even possible to feel what she was feeling. Now he was nibbling at her chest, then moved to press his face into her stomach.

Now her breath was in gasps! A crazy warm/hot flush was spreading all over from where his lips met her flesh. She moaned, and he slipped up. She clung to him, and kissed him hard. She wanted him *now*!

He chuckled, and pressed her face lightly against his chest. She kissed his nipples, and moved to lightly bite all over him. He did the same to her.

She wanted him *now*! At the same time she didn't want this to ever end. Her whole body was radiating heat, but it was a warm, inviting heat.

He raised up to kiss her very lightly, then....

"Hi! How are you this morning?" he greeted her. She laughed, and pulled him close. He made the low throaty chuckle, kissed her, and held her so tightly for a minute it was almost painful, then was moving against her, and she was pressing ever harder against him.

Afterward, he kissed her again, and got up to head for the bath, saying he was going to be late for work, but the boss would have to live with it.

High steel workers were not standing around looking for jobs. He came out and dressed, then she went in. He had eggs, bacon, and toast ready, when she came out. They finished the breakfast, and she said she had to change and get to work, herself.

"Tonight?" he asked, smiling, as she went across to her apartment.

"Oh, yes!" she replied.

She had never believed before that there would be much difference in her feelings when she "became a woman." Brother! Had she been wrong!

The next night was a fantasy. There were a lot of things she'd heard about, but hadn't dared to think she would ever do. Decent women did *not* do those perverted things.

She did a couple. She couldn't believe how she felt. Decency could go to hell! When he moved his huge powerful hands around her body, she returned the pleasure, then was kissing places she definitely knew no decent woman would ever come close to.

She was depraved. She didn't want to ever again be anything else.

One thing her mother had gotten through to her was that one did things with a husband she would never consider doing with anyone *not* a husband.

A decent woman would die before doing those depraved, perverted things.

If this was perversion, bring it on!

Her mother always warned that a man knew when a woman was wanton, and would never allow her the chance to become a decent woman again. Men *knew*.

Perhaps it was true. She was suddenly a center of attention for all the men she knew were always looking for a quick piece of ass.

Funny. She was thinking in patterns and ways she never had before. She began to even give speculative look at some of the men, though most disgusted her. She had a man who took care of himself. These pencil-pushers were flabby and soft. She already had what fifty of them couldn't give her.

It was nice to know it was there, anytime she wanted it. In quantity. She might question the quality, but that Sam Dells spent two night a week at the gym. He had a body almost as exciting as Tom's. It might be a fun experience, but she wouldn't chance ruining what she had.

That night she tried a few other things she had heard about. Tom had a video of a lot of things that she wouldn't do, and some she definitely would. Tom had things he wanted that she didn't, particularly, but she was willing to do them, if he would make the same concessions to her. She found that some things she thought she wouldn't like, she did.

Four weeks of bliss, then she came home early from work one afternoon to discover there was another woman in Tom's apartment. It hurt her, a bit, but she figured what's good for the gander is good for the goose, and changed to go out and to the gym to ask about using the place to keep in shape. Sam Dells just "happened" to be there (she had waited until he came in. It was a regular night for him). She went up to the registration desk as he was talking to the man sitting there, and said hello. They chatted a moment, then Sam said he'd better get his session over with.

She said maybe they could have a beer or something after the session.

He said his boyfriend wouldn't much like that. Live and learn!

She went back to her apartment. Tom came to ask why she was so late. She said she had come in earlier and found that he was busy, so she went out.

He said he never made any commitment. She knew that, and had agreed.

"I know. I'm not tied to you, and you're not chained to me."

He knew it was over. So did she.

Well, maybe a friendly romp when they were both in the mood.

She went to bed, alone. She thought a lot about it.

In a way, her mother had been right. Trouble was, it fit a hundred years ago. It didn't fit now.

She had to get a refill on the pills. She also had to be careful. There were some pretty horrible things around.

Her mother had been right about that, too. Once you start, you turn into a total wanton, almost overnight.

That might not be so bad!

Artie Hill was almost as goodlooking as Sam. She held out for a week, then happened to see him at the Nightowler Café. They had a couple of cups of coffee, and he suggested they go to Barney's Barn for a drink. She ended up spending the night at his place.

Big disappointment! No foreplay, hardly at all! What the guys called a "Slam-bam-thank-you-m'am!" One time, then he turned over and went to sleep. In the morning, he said they would have to get together again, sometime. Maybe a lot of times!

She shrugged, and said she had to get to work.

One time with someone like him was one time

too many.

The next Saturday night, she went to that Level Three Bar and Lounge, on Eighth. It was a lot of out-of-shape men in their late twenties to their late fifties who thought any woman who glanced their way was hot for them.

Look in a mirror, for god's sake! Look around! Why in Hell would a woman get hot for something like you!

She was just behind a guy who looked like he could use some exercise to give him the strength to carry that beer gut around. He was describing the only kind of woman who turned him on:

"She has to be trim, you know? Nothing turns me off so fast as a fat broad. She has to be clean. There has to be a chemistry, you know? Like, when she looks in your eyes hers are saying, 'You could be the one who could teach me something!' She's got to have a good body. I said that. I like nice large boobs and a thin waist and long smooth legs. A woman who takes care of herself, and doesn't turn into a frump as soon as she hooks some idiot.

"And her teeth! I can't take those yellow teeth. She can't smoke. Tobacco turns me off faster than fat. Long hair. Real blond, you know? Somebody you want to be seen with. Somebody who will make all you hangers-around jealous!"

He saw a buddy grin at her, and turned around.

"And here she is! What's your name, Honey? I was just describing the type of woman I can't resist, and here you are!"

She felt evil. "Oh? I heard part of it. You're looking for a woman who's everything you're not.

"Tell me. Why would a woman with even half the qualities you're looking for even bother to look in your direction? What in Hell do you have to offer to a woman who could snap her fingers and have anyone she wanted in this place – not that there would be anyone she wanted in this place?"

"Ooh! You're a feisty one, aren't you?" he reached toward her.

"If you touch me, I'll cut it off for you and make you eat it! Capich?"

He stopped, and looked both mad as hell and a little scared.

"Shit! I'll bet you haven't had it up in a year! You're like a frog. All belly, except for the head, and that's all mouth! Like Juan says, 'Habla mucho, dice nada.' Take a hike!"

She got up, and walked out. She could hear his buddies ragging at him. One said she had him pegged, to the last detail. He took a swing at the guy, who ducked, and came up to hit him in the mouth.

She sighed, and went to Harry's. She didn't care to stay around to watch the brawl she had instigated.

She should have gone to Harry's, in the first place. There were two guys who *did* look great! They seemed very nice, and it was plain they wanted to have a little fun, but made it as plain they weren't looking for a steady girlfriend, or anything.

She wasn't sure she was ready to be with two guys at once, but got a little drunk, and went with them to the Trucker Stop Hotel.

She had a very good time. They were fun, and they showed her a couple of things that took three. She had seen it on a video at Tom White-cloud's place. In the morning, she left. These guys said they had as good a time as they ever had. They would look her up, next time they came through. They drove big rigs, coast-to- coast.

She was thinking about it as she went back to her place to change for work. Those were really great guys, but there was something missing. Had she made a big mistake by going with an Indian first? Were those women right when they said an Indian would make other men seem second-rate?

Bill and Dan were great. She definitely would like to spend a night with them, now and then –

stuff, and Dan could handle the live performance part.

She was made a true fan when they did the old Janis Joplin piece, *Little Piece of My Heart* as trade-off lines. They, as she was prone to say, tore it up. They found a permanent audience, right there. Their voices were the perfect blend. Dan could get a growl, with just short of a whine, and Marie could do Janis very well. They were going places! Definitely!

The show broke up at four twenty in the morning. Jimmie and Lucy got in his truck and headed for her place.

"What did you think?" Jimmie asked.

"I think I'm in heaven! I never saw that much talent on one stage before, and I went to a lot of concerts by the biggest groups! Dan and Marie are going places!"

"Well, they do some good stuff. Dan should write more, and Marie less. She tends to the more dated things. If those things she wrote were in the early seventies, they would have been really big.

"On the other hand, Marie should sing more, and Dan less. They should make most of their stuff duets. They contrast."

"I have to agree. Overall, they're a refreshing change to what music has become."

"No. The music's still there. What will

probably happen to Dan and Marie is that they play the bars and small concerts. They won't get any promotion. Music has become just another commercial venture that depends on formulas. They don't fit. They're better than that, so they won't get backing, but they'll be a really big cult team. The guys are from that era, and a little later. They know not many will get the breaks Striker Run got. Striker went to the formula. They sound just like fifty other bands out there. The result is that they make a ton of money, and music suffers. Dan and Marie can't go formula. They don't fit."

"Jimmie, you scare Hell out of me!"

"I do? Why?"

"We think too much alike. Everything about you is too perfect."

There was a silence. "Me, too, to tell the truth. I don't know if I'm ready."

They rode along in silence until they got to her apartment. Jimmie pulled up in front of the side entrance. He didn't stop the engine. Lucy didn't say a word. She got out, went around to the driver's window, and leaned to kiss him. It lingered.

It lingered some more.

"What the Hell! Neither one of us can fight this!" He turned off the engine, and got out.

Lucy pressed her face into Jimmie's stomach, to lay like that, unmoving, for a minute. He lightly caressed her hair. She moved up to have her lips against his chest. She sighed. He ran his hand lightly along her back.

This much heaven wasn't possible. She remembered how, just shortly before, they had been one. It wasn't possible for two bodies to merge into one like that, but she had experienced it. She had never been able to stop thinking altogether before for more than a few seconds, but this merging was without thought. It was waves of pleasure that went on and on. Not one word in her thoughts. Not one picture. A floating in a sea of intense sensation that was Jimmie.

Well, maybe her friends were right. Maybe sleeping with an Indian would leave her unable to want anything else. It only almost happened with Tom. It was here with Jimmie. It was real. She couldn't picture her wanting any other man. Even Lance, as fantastic as he was, couldn't hope to come close to Jimmie.

"Should I move here, or will you want to move to my place?" Jimmie asked. "Stupid! You can walk to work from here, and I have my truck. Jadia can move into my place. She can save the rent, that way.

"Will you want to start a family right away, or

wait until we're more secure?"

"Wait, but not too long."

He didn't have to say anything. They had the rest of their lives.

They stayed there as long as they could, just being together. Lucy finally got up, used the shower, and slipped on a robe, to cook a cheese omelet and coffee. Jimmie came in, and made some fried bread to go with it. They didn't need conversation. Just being close was enough.

Could this possibly last?

She was damned well going to find out!

After another half hour, Jimmie had to get to his place to change into work clothes, and Lucy had to open the office. All the arrangements were made, without words, to a great extent. Jimmie would put his things in the truck and bring them home after work tonight.

This was now home. His house was where his niece was living.

Nan and Lance came in, bringing Lonnie, about nine thirty. She asked how the trip to the city went.

"Very well, really," Lonnie replied. "We got a lot of things settled. Company things."

Nan looked impish. "Did you two manage to sleep together?"

"Yep!" Lance quickly said. "We didn't get a lot

of sleep, though!

"Anything interesting for you, Luce?"

"Well, in a way. I went to Denton with Jimmie, for the show. It was really great! We didn't get back here until nearly daylight!

"Oh! Yeah! I got married, so it's over between us. You have Lonnie, so that's alright."

Nan said, "You aren't kidding, are you? You really did get married."

"In my heart, yes. Jimmie and I just meshed. I always knew it would happen, someday, but didn't expect it for another couple of years, but things happen when they happen. We'll be married officially when we have the time."

"Nothing meshed with Lonnie and me, so I'll have to keep looking. You said you considered marriage to be the end of screwing around, so I don't need to try."

"You're a wonderful person, Lance. I do love you, but I'm *in* love with Jimmie."

"I guess that means I'll never know if he would like a romp with me or not," Lonnie complained.

"If he was only in the pitcher's box."

"Shit! That's the way I want it!"

They joked until Laura Wright came in to pay her bill. She said she saw Jimmie's truck by Lucy's gate. Be careful! She'd heard those Indians could make a woman crawl around their feet without trying!

"That, I can tell you, is absolute truth!" Lucy responded.

They joked awhile, then everyone went his or her own way.

Lucy felt guilty. Nobody deserved perfection. She had found it. Here was a place where she fit, where she was close to so many people. None of it was the false front of the city.

Would it continue? Was she in for a huge crash?

Only time would tell.

but she would drop them in a heartbeat if it was them for a lot of nights or Tom for one.

Okay. He was first, and he was special, for that. Unlike what some had told her, he made it very special, that first time. She could picture if it had been Artie. She would have turned out as frigid as her mother!

Not true, but she would definitely not be out looking for anything. It would only happen after she got drunk, or whatever, not before.

She noticed people as she walked home, the five blocks. There was that thing on TV about the fattening of America. Brother, was that true! Eighty or ninety percent of the people she saw, women and men, were fat and out of shape! Those fat, ugly ... pigs! ... would give her the "Come-on" eye contact. She could vomit! She couldn't even picture it!

There were several new black people checking into her apartment building. That didn't hold true to them. To the men. The women were getting a little too plump.

She wondered if it was true about the blacks. They certainly seemed to have great bodies!

Well, maybe she'd learn, before long, if they were as great in bed as Sandra, Billi, Jean, and Carol said. For now, she was going to be late if she didn't get her ass in gear!

It was Saturday night, again. She had spoken with the new tenants, a little. They seemed nice enough. The women weren't wives, they were sisters. They were in one apartment, the men in another. She was going past when "Stake" was coming out of the apartment. She said "Hello," and chatted a minute, then went on. Stake made it plain he wanted her, but no more that close. Tom went by, and they always spoke, but it left a little ache inside.

She went to several places, but there wasn't anyone she would give the time of day to. She was becoming almost obsessed with finding a guy who wasn't a weaklooking out-of-shape slob. She talked with a couple who were presentable, but they came across as jerks. They knew they were what a lot of women looked for, and seemed so self-centered she knew it would be a disaster. A roomful of Arties. Yuck!

She went back to her apartment early. Stake was standing in his doorway, and stopped her. He invited her inside for some coffee – or whatever.

What the hell? Why not? It would be a good night to find out!

It was a disaster! He told her the coffee was on the stove. Bring him a cup. Cream and two sugar.

She bit back a retort. It was a cultural difference, probably. She got the coffee. She had to wash the cups and saucers. The dishes were all dirty, and in the sink.

She went back, and he was sitting there, nude. She stopped, looked at him, holding the hot coffee.

"On your knees, bitch!" he ordered.

She dumped the hot coffee in his lap, he screamed, she ran out.

She should have known. He was always sort of posing when she had seen him, before. He was just like those others at the bars. He thought all he had to do was snap his fingers, and the women would do anything he wanted. He was good-looking, and knew it.

He was also a total asshole! She hoped the coffee burned him enough that he wouldn't be able to have sex for a month! Didn't it register on him at all that he wouldn't have been there alone if a tenth of the women he thought wanted him wanted him?

Rap. She had seen exactly that kind of fantasy attitude over and over on those rap videos, though a lot of the performers were fat ugly pigs that had no talent, whatever, who spouted horrible poetry to a non-beat. If they didn't have all those three-quarters naked sexy bimbos hanging on them and shaking in the videos they wouldn't sell two copies of anything they did – and those two to relatives.

Want to admit the truth? This world has totally gone to Hell. We're on the back side of Armageddon. God lost! We are now living in Hell, and didn't know it!

She went to bed.

In the morning, she saw Carol, in the employee's lounge. Carol said she had gone by, and saw she had two *gorgeous* new neighbors. She would know by now that what they said about black men was true!

"I would? I haven't seen where they're any different than anybody else. That Stake character is a total asshole! I guess, if you're willing to put up with that 'On your knees, bitch!' type you might find them sexy, or whatever. I find them disgusting and repulsive!"

"But that's part of it! A strong man who knows what he wants and, not asks, *demands* it! It's sexy as all Hell!"

"Maybe to you. Not to me! I'm not into the bondage bit. At all! You want him, all you have to do is walk by his door. He's convinced himself that any woman who gets a glance at him is in love. Shit!

"It might be a good idea to wait a week or so. It seems he spilled hot coffee in his lap, and got his balls scorched! I doubt he'd be able to do you any good like that."

"Really? Do you know what he'll do?"

"Nothing. I do have friends who'll make him beg to let him die."

"Oh, girl! Have you got a lot to learn! You do *not* play that game with that kind! He'll just get ob ... you'll find out!"

She swore, and went to her job.

Stake was standing in his doorway when she went home. She asked how his sex life was, now that he didn't have one.

"Mama, you are a cool one! You know you got whatever you want. I'll do the knees bit for you, or anything else. Ain't nobody ever backed me down before. I got to have you! I'll go crazy if I can't have you! Please! I'll crawl and beg! Anything you want!"

"After that stunt? Are you nuts! Get a life!"

"Ooh, Mama! Hurt me! I gotta have it!"

"Gah! You ... Gah!"

She went to her apartment. She locked the door, and started to undress. There was a knock.

"Who? What?"

"I'm your slave forever, Mama! Please let me in! I won't do nothing! I swear! I need you, Mama!"

"Go away!"

"Don't make me break down the door! I'll just get in trouble! I need you!"

She grabbed the phone, and called the police. Stake was at the door, begging her to let him in, just to talk.

He started hitting the door with something. She picked up a big kitchen knife, and stood, scared half out of her wits. There were sounds, then a voice that called, "Police! Don't move!"

"Oh, God! I wasn't doing nothing! She drives me crazy! I wouldn't touch her! I gotta be where I can see her! Oh, *God*!"

"Ma'am? You alright in there?"

"Yes. Please! Just make him leave me alone! Stay away from me!"

There was a scuffling, then quiet. She took a very deep breath, then went to the door.

She changed her mind. She was *not* going to open that door!

Ten minutes later, "Ma'am? Police. I have to speak with you."

She opened the door, with the knife in her hand.

"Ma'am, he would take that away from you in a flash. He'll be in the cell for forty eight hours, then we have to let him loose, if he hasn't actually harmed anyone. I know the type. He'll come straight here. He can be dangerous. He's a crackhead. They're unpredictable."

"What can I do? I don't want anything to do with him!"

"I know I'd just move. He'll never stop. He's obsessed. You're the first woman who ever stood up to him. He thinks you own him, or he's in love, or something. It's the drugs, and the fact he's nutzo, anyway. Probably steroids and drugs. That's how he acts."

"I can't just move! I can't afford it! Oh, God!"

"Well, you could get someone to live with you for a couple of weeks. He'll be out of here, by then. I also know that much about those druggie punks! He'll have to run from someone, or he'll end up a statistic on the unsolved murder list."

"I don't think any of the girls would take the chance and live with me. They would be as afraid of him as I am!"

"I didn't mean a girl. That wouldn't even slow him down."

"You mean to have some guy move in?"

"You gotta do what you gotta do. It's, as Joe Walsh said, survival in the city."

"Who in Hell is Joe ... like I care! The only guys I would move in are two truck drivers who are in New York, by now, and an Ind ... friend, who already lives close. Maybe him. I can ask. Maybe I could move in with him. That might be a lesson that creep could learn!”

“He’s a creep? Oh! You mean Stake. I doubt it. Crackheads never learn anything.”

“I’ll think of something. I’m really sort of sick of this place. It’s just hard to find anywhere, now. Nothing I can afford. I got this place cheap, and can stay until I leave at the price, but anything ... you know how that works.

“Thanks, officer. I really do appreciate your help.”

He saluted, and started to walk away, then turned. “You got a deadbolt for that door?”

“Yeah. I’ve never used it. Now, there ain’t gonna be anytime I’m here when I *don’t* use it!”

“Good thinking.” He went on down the stairs. She closed the door, and shot the two deadbolts. She went to look out the window. The officer was just getting to the car. He called, and another, younger officer came from the building to get in the driver’s side. He looked like he had a body that would ... what the Hell!? Three minutes after something like that, and she was looking at men again?! She was as sick as Stake!

She sighed. She had to think of something. She had to get away!

That wouldn’t be a problem, in some ways. She certainly had had enough of the city!

Her father had once taken her and her mother

to a place to the southwest. A little sleepy town that she remembered as being dull, in a nice way. Her mother said it could be the place they wrote that Peyton Place book about! Don't let that facade fool you!

Did anyone else remember that stupid TV show? She noticed that her mother wouldn't miss a re-run on that channel 500, or something. It was purely stupid, to her.

Her mother had never been realistic about sex. Her father ... well, *duh*! For the first time in her life she connected things she'd heard. Her father was, to be kind, less than well-endowed, to the point he was a joke. Her mother wasn't frigid so much as she was disappointed! She was too religious to go out and find someone who could satisfy her, and hid it behind pretending to not like sex! She was married, and thought she would go to Hell if she got a divorce or had a lover!

Result: she lived in a homemade Hell her whole life since marrying her father

Your daughter isn't going to let that happen to her!

She sighed. Maybe it would be fun to live in Peyton Place. She had enough to live a little while put away. A place could be the same as anything else. If you don't like it, get the Hell away from it!

She made a quick phone call. Yes, there was a bus, four times a day, that went through Marbleville.

She ordered a ticket, and started packing. There wasn't a lot to take with her. Two large suitcases and two carry-on things. She was booked on the six thirty bus.

She called the night girl at work and said she was in great danger, and had to leave. She'd get in touch about the job and what she was owed and such.

Marbleville

Lucy got off the bus and stretched. It was a lot like she remembered from the visit, eight years ago.

First things first. The only hotel was the Grand Oaks, and it was only about ten rooms. It was just two blocks from where she got off the bus. She got one of the two cabs in the town to take her there. She got a room for the night – just eighteen dollars! She had planned on things costing what they did in the city! This was less than half, and was fairly nice, not a fleabag, like thirty five dollars would get in the city!

There was one real estate office, just one block back on the main road. She would get a meal, and see if she could get an apartment for what she was paying in the city, though she knew she had a good deal there. Just eight fifty and electric and water. She was able to get it for what the leaving tenant got if for, ten years ago, or something. *Don't* get your hopes up!

Well, hopes, but be realistic.

The hotel had a little restaurant. It seemed a popular place for the locals. She got the grilled chicken. There were no prices on the menu, but it wouldn't be over fifteen dollars, surely. There were items with a price, such as *French Fries one dollar extra*. She thought that might be a bit stiff, but saw a plate of fries on a table, two away. There were four people, and the fries were in a basket that served all four. She noted the signs that said no MSG was used there. She had read some things that suggested the stuff wasn't good for the health, but that it did make food taste better, and was a shortcut that so-so cooks used. Good cooks didn't need it. The natural flavors were better – if the cook knew how to bring them out.

She found the chicken had a very distinct and *good* flavor! Sort of Italian. She asked the waitress if it was a secret recipe.

"I don't think so. I'll ask Mabel."

She came back with a piece of paper with the recipe on it! Oregano, garlic, sweet basil, black pepper, and celery seed! Use dill, and a little vinegar. <u>Very little salt.</u>

She got the check, and asked if there was a mistake. She got a whole meal. The bill was seven fifty. Was it supposed to be seventeen fifty?

"Lunches are seven fifty. This isn't one of those rip-off fancy-schmancy places, like Routers, where iced tea is two dollars. It's plain old good food."

"I'll very certainly be eating here regularly!"

She had lucked out, again!

She went to the Green Acres Realty office. Yes, they had a few apartments for rent, and a few houses. Apartments were all prices, from two hundred thirty a month to more than five hundred. Would she be sharing, or alone? In town, or more to the outskirts?

"Fairly close, I suppose." *Five hundred? What? A chicken coop?*

"We have one that is quite nice. It's not large. One bedroom, a bath, a kitchen, a washroom, and a living room. It doesn't have a dining room, but the man who lived there used the little balcony for a dining area.

"It's a little pricey, but I think you would like it."

A little pricey – at half what she paid in the city?

"Are electric and water separate?" She felt she had to ask something, not just yell, "Sold!" Water and electric were always extra.

"Well, water is extra, but electric and gas are included. The water will cost four twenty per month."

"Well, I'll look at it. It might do. How much?" She was having a hard time not dancing on the desk!

"Er, Three fifty. I know it sounds expensive, but it is nice, and in a good section."

Christ Almighty, damn! Yes! Sold!

"I figured right about that. If it's nice, I'll probably take it." *Sold! Sold! I'll take it! Sold!*

"I'll have Lance show it to you. He's my son. We live in that area, so you know it's a good section. I could get a place anywhere, in this business."

She made a phone call, and said Lance would be there in about ten minutes. He would show her the place. If she liked it, he would help her take her things there. She discussed raising a son without a father. The father died twelve years ago, of cancer. She tried not to be too doting a mother.

The way the woman talked, Lance would be about fifteen years old, and a boy that mother had coddled all his life. Nancy (everyone calls me "Nan") Longton, the agent, was about fifty, and the motherly type.

A fancy '77 Goat, perfectly restored, eggshell blue, pulled up out front. A tall, slender man of about twenty five came in, to be introduced as Lance. He had beautiful blue-grey eyes, was blond, with hair a bit longish. He had what she referred to as a "Surfer" body. He was wearing a muscle shirt and tight pants, both of which he filled to perfection. His smile was beautiful. Teeth that had to have ten thousand dollars worth of dental work to be that perfect, but Nan never was in a position to afford that, so it was just natural perfect teeth. Lucy felt a bit weak in the knees. Nan was in the little closet, getting the keys. Lance raised an eyebrow at her. She definitely hoped he wasn't going to be another Artie! If he was half of what Bill or Dan were, she was going to enjoy the Hell out of Marbleville!

What was wrong with her? She just got there, three hours ago, he was the first really attractive man she met – and she was horny, all of a sudden?

Lance took the keys, and waved for Lucy to get in the car. They drove about five blocks away, and he stopped in front of a red brick house with white trim that should have been on a postcard! Big trees in the side yard – one dripping with apples! Pink and white Seven Sisters Roses on the porch rail. Huge Peppermint Stripe peonies at the corners.

"The apartment is the little cabin in back. It's kind of nice, and is private. There's an entrance on the road to the side, but I bring people to the front so the Adams won't think anyone is sneaking in. If you like the place, you can come and go from back there, and no one will know when – or with whom, not that the Adams would notice. We believe in the right to privacy, here. When and where anyone goes is nobody's business.

"That's with the standard gossips, on the side. They'll talk about what a tramp you have to be because no one looks as good as you who isn't a tramp! Small town crap!"

He grinned, and winked. She grinned back. She certainly hoped *he* would be coming. Often!

They went around the curving brick path to a perfect little two story fairytale house. It was half again the size she'd thought it would be.

"Downstairs is a garage and big storage place. That's part of the deal. I keep telling Mom it isn't expensive when you consider you get that. The storage alone would cost twenty bucks at the place by the main road.

"The furniture is mostly just the essentials. The TV isn't the newer type. Just an older flat twenty nine inch, but it's not really part of the deal. You can use it, or they can junk it, if you have your own. Cable is extra. Nine ninety five for basic. Most people go for the basic plus, which is fourteen, but you get a hundred channels, so everything's on it. Pay per is your own decision.

"Internet is included for six bucks a month

more."

"This place would be two grand in the city. I'll take it."

"Before you've seen inside – or tried out the bed and stove, or whatever?" He grinned the sexy grin. She raised an eyebrow, and said she was sure the bed would do fine. She would try it out, but this was the kind of place she knew would meet her expectations. The eyebrow was just as she said, "Expectations."

He laughed, and said he always set his expectations low, so any surprises would be for the better!

They went inside. It was a very comfortable room, larger than she expected. Very clean and well-kept. She checked out the place and the little balcony that overlooked the apple tree and side yard.

She went back in and to the bedroom. She sat on the bed, and said the mattress was perfect, as she knew it would be.

He sat beside her. "I'm not good at making propositions. You turn me on, big time! Want to test the bed to be sure it's what you want?"

"The bed's not what I want, right now! You're what I want, right now!

"I don't believe I said that! I've never done anything like this before! Wow!"

He laughed, and kissed her. She bit at his shoulders, and he fumbled at her blouse. She slipped out of the blouse and dropped the bra. He was biting and licking. She dropped the skirt, and slipped out of the panties as he unbuckled his pants and slipped out of the muscle shirt.

His body was as perfect as Tom's! She was nibbling at his chest and running her tongue all over him. He slipped around, and was nibbling at her chest, at the same time. They moved lower and lower.

She had never done anything like this before! It was what the CDs Tom had called a sixty nine. She hadn't thought she'd really go for that, but it was pure heaven!

Then the "regular" way. They were both almost exhausted. He said they ought to try out the shower, or his Mom would catch on – not that she didn't already know there was some chemistry, from in the office. She had to act like she thought her son was a virgin around others, though she had talked over things with him, and had warned him about certain things. She was a person you could talk about anything with.

She laughed. "A virgin?"

"Not since I was about fourteen." They both laughed.

They went to the shower. It was a fun bath!

Lucy paid for first and last month, and Lance brought her things from the hotel. It was dinnertime, and she insisted on buying him and Nan a good meal. The three of them cost about what she would have paid for herself, alone, in the city, and the food was much more and much better prepared. Inez, the waitress, treated the customers like family. It was relaxed and comfortable.

They chatted awhile. Lucy said this town was just perfect for her, but she would have to find a job. That could be a problem.

"What kind of work have you done?" Nan asked.

"I was a secretary to a business executive, and have some training in that kind of thing, and I worked as a ticket agent at the bus terminal for a couple of months. I would have to leave the job before long. Gordon was getting around to the 'special duties' bit. I was definitely not interested. Not *him*!"

"Married?" Lance asked.

"Yes. Not to mention he was a fat sloppy pig! I couldn't even picture it! I couldn't picture it with about anybody there. Sixty male employees, and not but one who could interest me – and he was gay!"

"I have some gay friends," Lance said. "They

seem to attract the women, but don't want them. I don't get it, but everybody's different."

"We used to say, 'Everybody to his own bag.' Shows my age!" Nan said. "You ever make it with any of them, Lance?"

"Lonnie. From my end only."

"Lonnie? I'll forgive you for that. He's very nice, and very clean. I *thought* he was gay!"

"It was okay. Not my thing, either. You ever make it with any of your lesbian friends?" Lance asked.

"I've thought about it. It's not my thing. I don't think I would like it. Don't care to find out.

"You ever make it with a girl, Luce?"

"No. Same. Not my thing. I was raised to think I'd go to Hell if I ever even let it cross my mind." She couldn't believe a mother would ask her son about a gay relationship, particularly with a stranger sitting there! She couldn't believe she'd get an honest answer, if she did! Her experience with her mother was that decent people didn't discuss such personal matters. Her "sex education" was strictly the dry basic mechanisms and avoiding disease and pregnancy taught in school.

She liked these people. They were open and honest. They were playing with her head, and she knew it, but it was in fun.

After about an hour of them playing with her and her getting into the spirit of it, she said she was tired. She would start looking for a job, in the morning, but needed some sleep. Just to be devilish, she asked, "Lance, would you care to help me through the night?"

Nan burst out laughing. Lance joined her, then got in the one-up bit. "I thought that was decided when we met!" They said "Good night!" to Nan and went to the apartment. The first night there was fantastic!

Lance made a call before he left, in the morning. He said she might be able to get a job at the electric company. She had experience as a ticket agent, and it was a lot like that. The bill had a bar code, she ran it through a machine, it gave everything she needed.

"A close friend, Lonnie Marks, is general manager. I think he'll be easy to work for ... I mentioned him last night. He definitely won't be trying to get in your pants. He's goodlooking, but he doesn't go for the straight bit, much. I'll tell him you know he's gay, and don't think it makes a shit. He's just your boss, not a lover."

She laughed. "That's a true statement!"

She puttered around the place for a couple of hours to get things where she wanted them. The furniture looked new, but she knew it was quality stuff, and taken care of. She would very definitely take as good care of it.

The electric company was just six blocks away. It was a small office with a counter and a cage with a window. Lonnie Marks was, as Lance suggested, very handsome. He had a great personality. He seemed a bit nervous, at first. She told him Lance had spent the night with her – he was a dream! – and that she knew he was gay. That was a blessing he couldn't know!

Or she thought it was. She was used to fat ugly pigs making cutesies sexual remarks. She didn't know he was going to be one she wished would! They started joking. Lonnie said he would slit his wrists for Lance. He was a god, walking! He was also the best bed partner he ever knew – don't let him know he said that! He didn't go with him, much, only when it was a longer dry spell. Most of the women here who weren't afraid because whatever you do is all over town before you get home were married. Lance would *not* lay a married woman!

"It's a joke. He says he doesn't do windows or married women."

"I don't get it?"

"Oh. Because a lot of the housemaids say they don't do windows. Part of small town terms. It's in their ads."

He showed her how to use the computers, and explained that there would be times when she would have to be a minor dispatcher, but that wasn't often. They had only the one regular crew, and they had the routine fixed. If there was a break or short or emergency she would have to radio to give them orders. They didn't come into town, unless called. They handled the whole county, and the "barn" was six miles out.

"The only one who gives Lance any competition with my desires is head of the crew. He's gorgeous! I think he might, but I don't know how their culture looks at it. Some friends say they aren't as negative as our own culture.

"I have some kind of thing. A dream that the tales are true, that they're better than us in the bedroom scene."

"They? You've lost me again?"

"The Indians. He's Apache.

"Oh! I should have told you his name. You'd have known it. Jimmie Blackeagle."

"The tales are damned well true, but Lance equals them. My first was with Tom Whitecloud. No one has measured up, until now."

"What about the blacks? Is it true they're the biggest, but are so sold on that they aren't worth the time in bed?"

"I can't say about most of them, but the one I almost went for turned out to be a nutcase crackhead with an ego problem."

A woman came in. Lonnie went through the bill payment process with her. It was easy.

She would start work at eight in the morning. While the pay wasn't what she was used to, the costs were so much less she actually came out better! A *lot* better!

She walked around the town for the rest of the day to learn where everything was. She noted that the men here, a great majority of them, took care of themselves. They weren't flabby and pale and weaklooking.

<u>*Coasting*</u>

Lucy smiled at Mrs. Winston, who was giving her a disapproving look. "What?"

"You come to this town from the city and corrupt our youth! You cannot expect honorable and decent people to accept your harlotry! You are damned! You will take our youth with you!"

"I didn't know that! What youth are you speaking of? I'm not aware of any youth I've corrupted. The only ones I've even met were here in the office, or at the grocery store. Doesn't leave much opportunity to corrupt, would you say?"

She had been warned about Mrs. Winston and four others, who were the super-pious type who spread gossip about anyone who didn't live their lives the way they thought it should be lived – which was 98 percent of the people.

"Lance Longton, for one! You are leading him straight to perdition! Yea! Satan's disciple!"

"Lance? He's six years older than me, so you can hardly say I'm corrupting the youth. Maybe he's corrupting me?"

"You are damned! I declare it! You are judged and found guilty! Amen!"

"What are you guilty of now, Lucy?" Nan asked, coming up behind Winston.

"Corrupting Lance, if I get what she's ranting about right."

"Good trick! He's a long way from being corruptible, by you or anyone else, I'm afraid. So now you are judged guilty. How interesting!

"Marta, I've warned you before about starting rumors about me or my family! Tread with care!"

"Well, she's judged me. I understand from my mother that God has made very strong warnings, himself, about those who would usurp his right to judge. I would suggest the first person here who needs fear perdition is the one who just acted in direct opposition to God's word, wouldn't you?

"I'm making no judgements, myself. It is only a question."

"You come here and, in two short weeks, begin to undermine our youth! You are damned!"

"Hi, Luce! What are you damned for, now?" Lance, who had come in close behind Nan, asked. Winston turned, and looked like a trapped animal.

"Corrupting you," Nan answered.

"Oh. That. I was corrupted a long time before I even met Luce.

"Luce, did Lonnie leave anything here for me? He said he was going to get some things when he went to the city yesterday." He winked at her, and added, "Some new sex toys and stuff like that."

Lucy looked innocent. "I think he left a box in the office. I'll get it."

"*Sex toys!?*" Winton squeaked.

"Yes. I'm going to give them to the kids at the high school. Part of the sex education classes you fought so hard to prevent," Nan said, choking back the laughter that was so plainly on her face.

"Yeek?!"

"Well, how could they learn anything, if all some teacher did was read from a book?" Nan asked.

Marta almost fainted. She was holding herself up on the counter.

"They aren't sex toys. They're connectors and insulators for rewiring the Donaldson place, and some heavier stuff. We're just trying to show you how silly you look to others with this oh-so-holy routine," Nan said. "I do mean it about you spreading your shit about me or my family. What Lance or Lonnie or I or Lucy or anyone else does is none of your damned business. I know very well what goes on with you and Parson Barber. I even a have a candid photo or two that were taken at the Easter party, by the lake."

"Yah...? You...?" She almost ran out.

"Well! I heard she and Barber were missing for

almost an hour, then. She sort of confirmed it, huh?"

"I doubt they did anything," Lance said. "Despite his faults, he's married, and believes in the sanctity, and all that."

"I heard she tried. He refused, and gave her some counseling, is all. She did have her blouse off. The Ford kids told me they saw that," Nan replied.

"Well, maybe that will shut her up," Lance said.

"Don't count on it!" Lucy warned. "I knew some of that type. My mother wasn't far from it, but she never got so extreme. Some of her friends could find something negative to gossip about if Jesus Christ came to town, I think.

"I was sort of baiting her."

"Well, this box is labeled for the crew, not me. I knew they would get it this morning and did a little baiting, myself. Jimmie or one of the crew will come for it before noon," Lance said. "Lonnie is in the city for a meeting of the company managers. I'm going to go. I'll spend the night there, and bring him back with me, in the morning."

"Going to spend the night with him?" Nana asked, a small grin on her face.

"Maybe. Depends on what's available."

They laughed, and chatted awhile. Some more people came in to pay their bills, and Nan and Lance left. Lucy waited on them, and chatted a few minutes. It was nice the way people would always stop for a little conversation, here. When they left. Carole Sanders came in. Lucy met her at the restaurant one night, and they were sort of pals.

"I was coming by about an hour ago, and saw the Winton pain-in-the-ass coming in, so waited. She had on her holier-than-thou face, so I guess she told you the shocking story about Sally and me. Hanging around the Router, trying to pick up anything in pants. Hallelujah and amen!"

"No. She came to announce I was judged and found guilty of corrupting the town's youth. Lance, for instance. I told her the Bible says that anyone who usurps God's right to judge is bound for Hell, so I'll probably see her there, or something."

"Lance? What a dream! A lot of us are jealous of your slutty ass for taking so much of his time!"

"He's one of the two men I've met who deliver the dream."

"Who's the other? Any chance I know him?"

"No. He's in the city. A high steel worker. Fantastic body, and the sexiest way of sort of growling in his throat. He's like Lance. He's as interested in getting me off as he is in getting off, himself."

"High steel? An Indian?"

"Uh-huh. It's damned true! Until Lance, that is."

A company truck pulled up, outside. A man who looked very much like Tom Whitecloud and another Latino-looking man got out.

"Speaking of sexy Indians, here's our local product. He's up to and exceeding national standards, I can attest!" Carole said. "Juan, with him, isn't far behind. I went with him a couple of times before he married Carmencita. He doesn't screw around. I respect him, for that. Most of the men here are out for anything they can get, married or not. You and I have already agreed that married men are out of the equation. We think alike, for that!"

Jimmie and Juan took a couple of crates from the truck, and brought them in. They introduced themselves to Lucy, and said the stuff was to be returned to the main warehouse. Lucy gave them the box Lance brought for them.

It was noon, so Lucy suggested they all go to the hotel for lunch. They agreed. It was a very pleasant hour, then Jimmie said they had to get back. A line was down on East Road. It was what the connectors were for. Carole said her goodbyes, and went toward her place. Juan got in the truck. Lucy was giving the invoice copy to Jimmie, who asked, "You and Lance got a steady thing?"

"We get along. No strings, or anything."

"Are you open for a date? – tell me to hike if it's too soon to ask."

"No. We have our own lives. I don't have a commitment, and neither does he. We both like to have a little fun, now and then. The possessive crap can make it no fun anymore. We both know it."

They agreed to meet tomorrow night. It was Saturday. Jimmie only worked until noon, unless there was an emergency call. The company offices closed at two, on Saturday. He would treat her to dinner, and they would find some entertainment. He didn't often go to bars, because he couldn't stop if he had a couple of beers. A lot of Indians had no resistance to alcohol.

"I don't much care for booze, myself. I'm not really a bar type."

"There's a live show in Denton. It's not far. I like that kind of thing sometimes," Jimmie said. "It's older musicians who retired from the commercial end, but like to get together. They write new stuff, and play it. A couple of big hits were from right there."

"What kind of music?"

"Everything from hard rock to country. A lot of ballads, like in the seventies and eighties. It's a lot of fun. When there's a local with talent, they include them. One group, Striker Run, is pretty big. Don and Jerry started right there."

"That sounds like heaven! I love that spontaneous kind of thing!"

He would pick her up at three. They would go out to the lake until around five, then go to The Experience Bar and Restaurant, in Denton, for the show. Shows lasted until anywhere from 9:30 to the next morning at daylight, depending on audience, who was there, and what they wanted to do. The early nights were usually because not enough showed up to perform – though one of them had stayed until daylight as a solo. He was that good.

Every day, Lucy loved Marbleville a little more.

She was worried, just a little. Jimmie seemed the type she would want to herself. That must not be allowed to get in the way of what could be a beautiful thing. While she fully planned to settle down with a one and only, it was far to early for that in her life.

The Experience

The lake was fun. They teased and played. They quickly learned to be at ease with one another. Neither was in a hurry to take it further. Lucy and Jimmie fit perfectly in personality and philosophy.

She met Arnie and Frieda Goldstein. They seemed a little out of the mood of the time and place. Jimmie later introduced her to Annette Goldstein, who Jimmie explained used to be the Mrs. Goldstein. Frieda Green was married to Morris Green, at the time. Arnie was married to Annette.

"They're the result of playing those stupid games. Frieda moved in on Arnie the minute they met. It managed to break up two marriages and make six people unhappy. Now Frieda's sneaking around with Bill Evers. Arnie was moaning about it to me. What could he do? How could she do that to him?

"I told him she had broken up him and Annette. She wanted the challenge to see if she could break up someone else."

"I have a stock answer to that type," Lucy said.

"If he or she will cheat *with* you, they'll cheat *on* you. Get over it. It's what you are."

"I believe, when you're married, that's it, for the screwing around. It's a matter of personal code. If you haven't found the right one, don't get married. Know when it's chemistry, and when it's more. If it's right, you won't be looking."

Lucy nodded. "We think exactly the same, there. I'm having fun and learning things, but won't marry a guy until I know full well he's the one.

"My mother married my father before she had any experience, whatever. The result was that she was almost frigid, and was never happy while he was alive. She hid her frustration in life behind her religion."

"There are more than a couple of those here!"

"I've met some of them."

They sat close, and talked. They got to the restaurant a little later than they had planned. It was crowded. It seemed a favorite was there with two people he found who wanted to see if they would click with an audience. They had done some things on video, and he thought they had what it takes. By morning, they would know.

The food was a little better than so-so, but the atmosphere made it delicious. People would stop to chat. A lot of them knew Jimmie. Two women were blatant about wanting Jimmie to spend the night with them. He said once was enough, with them. A beautiful Indian woman came to sit with them to talk. Jimmie introduced Jadia Silvercreek, his niece. She and he were centers of attention the whole night. A lot of men came to chat with Jadia. A lot of women came to chat with Jimmie. A couple of men, also. Men would come to chat with Lucy.

"I see there are some men who would like to get you in bed," Lucy said. "I know one who does, but he doesn't know if you go for that."

"It's different. I only play from the pitcher's box. Will you tell me who?"

"Lonnie."

"He seems very nice. I would think anyone that handsome would want both ends. I won't go that far."

They talked about other things.

The show started at about eight fifteen. Jack Stoner, the older man, simply went onto the stage, tuned his guitar, and said Dan and Marie Holt would try for the brass ring with them. He would play lead guitar, and Barry Black would do the drums bit. Marie would play keyboards and vocals, and Dan would play rhythm and vocals. This was an original thing Dan wrote for Marie, followed by one Marie wrote for Dan.

Stoner started with a melodic lead that broke into a rock beat when Marie sang:

Hold me!
Hold me 'til the fear subsides,
Hold me 'til there's noplace more to hide,
'Til hope is standing by my side, 'Til I can be no longer blind...
Tell me!
Tell me why this pain inside,
No longer serves to make me wonder why,
I can't begin to get you off my troubled mind.

Explosive power chords. Heightened drums. Bass (a man who had come onstage just as they started and plugged in) running counterpoint to rhythm.

You stand there now, when you never did before,
To try to make me think you still care for only me,
When I can see you're nothing but a lie, I cry....
Hold me. Tell me yet another lie.

Back to medium rock ballad.

Walk out,
Don't look back,
Don't say another word that would deny,
We both know that it's over now. No time to fake another vow

Goodbye.
Crying heavy lead. Repeat chorus.

It really was good. Lucy and the crowd agreed, with applause.

Dan moved to a vocals mike. The man on the bass took Stoner's guitar, and Stoner took the bass.

"Phil Martin on rhythm guitar and bass," Stoner announced.

Phil did a nice finger style bounce with a contrasting bass run. The drums were a folk beat. The rhythm was a strange off-country upbeat.

I know that I can not go back,
Along another railroad track,
Can't ride a boxcar anymore,
Can't take the hope that is no more,
I lived through Hell and heaven then,
I won't find bliss like that again,
I'll try. That's life, but there's something deep inside
That I will always seek, but never find.

A bluesy kind of chord run and a harmonica Lucy hadn't seen come on the stage.

You came into my life and it was fine.
You made this world a place that was all mine.
We spent a year in total bliss,
We'd start the day with one long kiss,
And then you simply went away,

I don't know why until this day,
I live my days in mem'ries of that year,
I wipe away a dream dropped in a tear.
A longer break with very good guitar work.

Lucy liked the song and arrangement. Very much. She didn't much like that last line, but it still fit, somehow. She thought about the symbolism. Maybe a dream dropped in a tear. *Wiped away* tear. It was pretty good, really.

So now I'll go along my road,
The one I've taken on my own,
Another unseen heavy load,
I'll walk along the way alone,
Another lane, another path,
Where maybe I'll try, or maybe cry,
I'll prob'ly try to bring a laugh,
The tears are gone, the mem'ries dry
A sobbing lessening run on the guitar, a wail from the harmonica. It struck Lucy how the rhyme scheme changed without changing the pattern of the song. It was really good, but Dan wasn't quite the right voice for it.

Love is one long unfunny joke.
That one was made by the musicianship and presence. It would be a lot like the old Grateful Dead things. Fantastic onstage, but a flop as a recording. Lucy was sure she would hear more about those two! Marie could handle the recorded

Lucy pressed her face into Jimmie's stomach, to lay like that, unmoving, for a minute. He lightly caressed her hair. She moved up to have her lips against his chest. She sighed. He ran his hand lightly along her back.

This much heaven wasn't possible. She remembered how, just shortly before, they had been one. It wasn't possible for two bodies to merge into one like that, but she had experienced it. She had never been able to stop thinking altogether before for more than a few seconds, but this merging was without thought. It was waves of pleasure that went on and on. Not one word in her thoughts. Not one picture. A floating in a sea of intense sensation that was Jimmie.

Well, maybe her friends were right. Maybe sleeping with an Indian would leave her unable to want anything else. It only almost happened with Tom. It was here with Jimmie. It was real. She couldn't picture her wanting any other man. Even Lance, as fantastic as he was, couldn't hope to come close to Jimmie.

"Should I move here, or will you want to move to my place?" Jimmie asked. "Stupid! You can walk to work from here, and I have my truck. Jadia can move into my place. She can save the rent, that way.

"Will you want to start a family right away, or

wait until we're more secure?"

"Wait, but not too long."

He didn't have to say anything. They had the rest of their lives.

They stayed there as long as they could, just being together. Lucy finally got up, used the shower, and slipped on a robe, to cook a cheese omelet and coffee. Jimmie came in, and made some fried bread to go with it. They didn't need conversation. Just being close was enough.

Could this possibly last?

She was damned well going to find out!

After another half hour, Jimmie had to get to his place to change into work clothes, and Lucy had to open the office. All the arrangements were made, without words, to a great extent. Jimmie would put his things in the truck and bring them home after work tonight.

This was now home. His house was where his niece was living.

Nan and Lance came in, bringing Lonnie, about nine thirty. She asked how the trip to the city went.

"Very well, really," Lonnie replied. "We got a lot of things settled. Company things."

Nan looked impish. "Did you two manage to sleep together?"

"Yep!" Lance quickly said. "We didn't get a lot

of sleep, though!

"Anything interesting for you, Luce?"

"Well, in a way. I went to Denton with Jimmie, for the show. It was really great! We didn't get back here until nearly daylight!

"Oh! Yeah! I got married, so it's over between us. You have Lonnie, so that's alright."

Nan said, "You aren't kidding, are you? You really did get married."

"In my heart, yes. Jimmie and I just meshed. I always knew it would happen, someday, but didn't expect it for another couple of years, but things happen when they happen. We'll be married officially when we have the time."

"Nothing meshed with Lonnie and me, so I'll have to keep looking. You said you considered marriage to be the end of screwing around, so I don't need to try."

"You're a wonderful person, Lance. I do love you, but I'm *in* love with Jimmie."

"I guess that means I'll never know if he would like a romp with me or not," Lonnie complained.

"If he was only in the pitcher's box."

"Shit! That's the way I want it!"

They joked until Laura Wright came in to pay her bill. She said she saw Jimmie's truck by Lucy's gate. Be carcful! She'd heard those Indians could make a woman crawl around their feet without trying!

"That, I can tell you, is absolute truth!" Lucy responded.

They joked awhile, then everyone went his or her own way.

Lucy felt guilty. Nobody deserved perfection. She had found it. Here was a place where she fit, where she was close to so many people. None of it was the false front of the city.

Would it continue? Was she in for a huge crash?

Only time would tell.

And Then...

"Hi, Mom! I just wanted to come by and let you be the first to know. I'm pregnant! You're going to be a grandmother in eight months and one week!"

"I thought so. I have a sort of feeling for that kind of thing," Lucy replied. "Your father and brother will be pleased for you, but won't show it, much. You know how men are.

"Come on in. I'll make a pot of coffee. Jimmie has a big bowl of fried bread, and I have a bowl of gravy. We can gossip about all our nutty neighbors."

"The only nutty neighbors around here are you and Dad. I would like some fried bread with that pineapple marmalade you make. And maybe some of that banana ice cream."

"Pineapple?! On fried bread?! See how I knew you were pregnant?"

They played and joked awhile, then Jani went back to her husband. Jimmie and Bob came in, soon. Lucy said Jani was pregnant.

"She'll be a good mother. You taught her well," Jimmie said. "Bob will probably make a good father, if he ever gets over the need of a new woman every night. He looks so Indian everyone thinks he has to live up to the reputation. It's such a duty!"

"All the way. I see Bob was at George's house night before last. Carey couldn't wait to tell me how he was headed straight for hell with the women, now he's heading for even worse, laying with homos!"

"Tell her I don't want to go to heaven if there are only people like her there!" Bob shot back. He waved, and went out to his car. He would be on the afternoon shift at the electric company. He was manager of the line crew, at nineteen years. His father taught him well.

Jimmie went to lay across the old comfortable oversized sofa. Lucy went to lay on him and press her lips to his chest.

It was still there. Beyond all possibility, they were still very much like they were when they first met, twenty three years ago.

The exception proves the rule.

C. D. Moulton's works are available on most major outlets as printed or e-books. CD writes the CD Grimes, PI, mysteries, the Det. Lt. Nick Storie mysteries, the Clint Faraday mysteries, the Flight of the Maita science fiction series, books on orchid culture and many others of many types. Mystery, adventure, intrigue, science fiction, humor, fantasy, paranormal, mild erotica, and factual.